Twas the Night Before HALLOWEEN

Written by Tim D. Welch
Illustrated by Matthew J. Delaney

Tim D. Welch

ISBN: 978-1-958842-06-5

Library of Congress Control Number: 2022941783

First Published by Spooky Ink an Imprint of AM Ink Publishing LLC, Southwick, MA 2022

www.AMInkPublishing.com

Twas the night before Halloween
and all through the house,

Every creature was stirring
even the old scary mouse.

The masks were hung by the door with fear,

In the hopes that the boogeyman would not come near.

The children were all hiding
under their beds,

With visions of monsters
dancing in their heads.

And mother with her
flashlight looking for the cat.

Who was hiding in the wall
to avoid a mean old rat.

When out of the window arose such a sound.
I crawled from my bed and tried to stay down

I creeped to the window just like a cat.
Hoping when I peeked out there was nothing spooky to look at.

The moon shined brightly on the ground below.
I noticed something that had a weird glow.

When what to my eyes did appear,
But eight tiny pumpkins lit up with fear.

There was a little old witch and a fiery pot,
I knew in that moment it had to be hot.

More rabid than a bat her coursers they came,
She whistled and shouted and called them by name.

Now ghost now goblins now skeletons and witches,
On spiders on centipedes on crickets and roaches.

To the top of the house and out of the wall,
Now slither away slither away slither away all.

The leaves blew in the haunting fall sky,
When they met up with the moon way up high.

So up to the top the coursers they flew,
With a bag full of scary and the boogeyman too.

With the screech of the banshee I heard on the roof,
She was haunting and scary and covered in goop.

As I drew my head and turned around,
I knew the boogeyman was inbound.

With a bag full of fright he flung over his back,
There was no telling the contents of that old dirty sack.

His eyes so creepy so empty so dark.
His cheeks like bone, his teeth like a shark.

His mouth so black and far from neat.
His breath smelled like two dirty feet.

The stump of his pipe in between his teeth.
Made the house smell like rotted beef.

He had a thin face and a little round belly,
That shook like a bowl full of Halloween jelly.

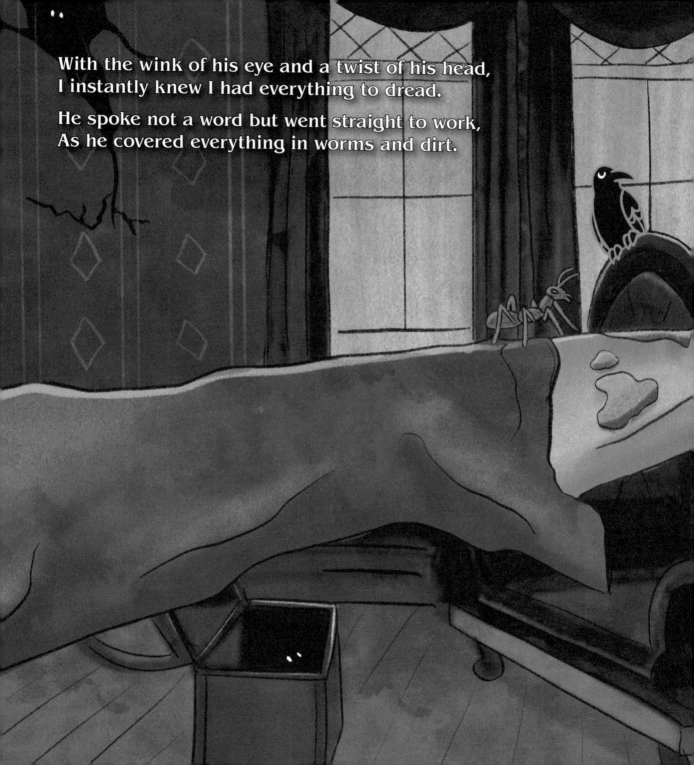

With the wink of his eye and a twist of his head,
I instantly knew I had everything to dread.

He spoke not a word but went straight to work,
As he covered everything in worms and dirt.

Laying his fingers across my lip,
telling me to shhhh as he tightened his grip.

With the blink of an eye he was gone.
Out the back door singing a song.

He sprang to his hearse and gave his team a whistle
And drove away like a speeding missile.

But I heard him exclaim as he drove off into the night
HAPPY HALLOWEEN to all and to all a haunted night.

DEDICATIONS

This book is dedicated to my grandpa BILL. A man who raised me. Grandpa and myself shared a love for Halloween, watching old scary movies and Halloween shows, as we sat and ate the seasonal Halloween candy that the stores would sell. Those memories to this day live on in myself and I was able to pass it down to my children. In school I loved Halloween because we would get the new books that would come out, the Halloween pencils, erasers, stickers, the decorations, the games we would play. Halloween has become such a huge part of my life over the past 45 years. I want to be able to share my love of Halloween with the world through my books. To bring back that nostalgic feel from when I was a child. Thank you Grandpa, I love & miss you very much, this book is for you and to keep our memories alive of a love we shared together.

Tim D Welch

I dedicate this book to my son, Kal-el. Always follow your dreams and remember that you can do anything you set your mind to. I love you to the full moon and back.

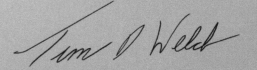

Matthew Delaney

CPSIA information can be obtained
at www.ICGtesting.com
Printed in the USA
LVHW071215021022
729744LV00033B/70